DATE DUE

JUL 30 2010		
GAYLORD		PRINTED IN U.S.A.

Surf's Up!

By K. C. Kelley

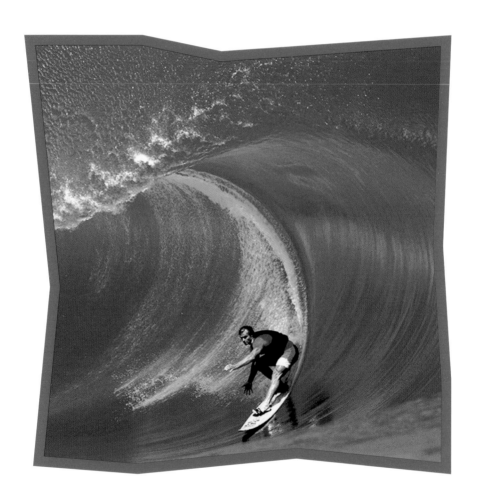

The
Child's
World®
www.childsworld.com

Published in the United States of America by The Child's World®
1980 Lookout Drive • Mankato, MN 56003-1705
800-599-READ • www.childsworld.com

ACKNOWLEDGMENTS

The Child's World®: Mary Berendes, Publishing Director

Produced by Shoreline Publishing Group LLC
President / Editorial Director: James Buckley, Jr.
Designer: Tom Carling, carlingdesign.com
Cover Art: Slimfilms

Photo Credits:
Cover: Corbis (main); Reuters (insets)
Interior: AP/Wide World: 5, 13, 19, 21, 24, 26, 29; Corbis: 15, 17;
Getty Images: 19, 20; GrantRohloff.com, 7; Reuters: 8, 10, 12, 23, 27

LIBRARY OF CONGRESS CATALOG-IN-PUBLICATION DATA

Kelley, K. C.
  Surf's up! / by K.C. Kelley.
    p. cm. — (Reading rocks!)
  Includes bibliographical references and index.
  ISBN 978-1-60253-103-1 (library bound : alk. paper)
  1. Surfing—Juvenile literature. I. Title. II. Series.

GV839.55.K45 2008
797.3'2—dc22

2008004485

CONTENTS

4   **CHAPTER 1**
Legends of
Surfing

16   **CHAPTER 2**
Surfer Girls

22   **CHAPTER 3**
Today's Surfing
Stars

30   **GLOSSARY**

31   **FIND OUT MORE**

32   **INDEX**

LEGENDS OF Surfing

"Catch a wave and you're sitting on top of the world!" That's what the California-born Beach Boys sang in the 1960s about the awesome sport of surfing. For hundreds of years, brave people have climbed onto surfboards and "caught" wave after wave.

Native people on South Pacific islands have been surfing for centuries. However, it was a Hawaiian Olympic swimming champion who made the sport famous around the world. Duke Kahanamoku

USA 34

DUKE KAHANAMOKU

2002

This U.S. postage stamp honored Duke for spreading the word on surfing. Duke also won three Olympic gold medals for swimming, and set two world records.

(kah-hah-nah-MOH-koo) won a gold medal at the Olympics in 1912. After the Games were over, he traveled the world in swimming **exhibitions**. He began to show off his surfing skills. People became more interested in this cool new sport—especially in Australia. By 1914, surfing was on the rise.

Surfing really became popular in the 1950s. Back then, the boards were long and heavy. Most boards were made of wood. People needed to be really strong to paddle them out into the surf!

The big change in surfing came in 1946, when the boards could be made of lighter plastic-like material. This could be shaped in many different forms, letting surfers do more tricks.

Among the early stars of the sport were Gerry Lopez, Greg Noll, and Miki Dora. They developed their skills on the giant waves of Hawaii's North Shore. They created new tricks almost every time they went out. They did the "hang 10," a trick in which they stood at the very tip of the board. They "carved" turns in waves. They "rode the tube" by shooting along the space under a curling wave.

These early surfers rode for the sheer joy of surfing, not for competition. But other surfers wanted to show off their skills, too. Competitions were created, and some people became **professional** surfers. The first star pro surfer was California's Corky Carroll. He won five U.S. championships in the late 1960s.

Miki Dora shows off a "hang 10" move. It's called that because the surfer has that many toes over the front edge of the surfboard!

Australian surfers ruled the waves in the 1970s and 1980s. Mark Richards was a four-time world champ during this time. He was famous for his smooth and **elegant** style. Fellow "Aussie" Tom Carroll followed Mark as world champ. Both men battled through injuries to stay at the top of the sport . . . and the waves!

In the early 1980s, however, a young American surfer emerged to break up the Aussies' run. Tom Curren grew up in Santa Barbara, California. His dad, Pat, was a famous surfer in the 1950s. Pat put Tom on a board as soon as he could walk!

By the time Tom was 17, he was winning **amateur** events. He won his first world title in 1985, and was champ again in 1986. After taking some time off to pursue his love of music, Tom returned to win another world title in 1990.

Tom is not competing anymore, but he still travels the world, looking for the perfect wave.

Aussie is a nickname for a person from Australia. It's usually pronounced "AUZ-zee."

Kelly Slater combines the moves of a gymnast with the style of a surfer.

Without a doubt, today's surfing king is Kelly Slater from the United States. No surfer has won as many world titles or become as much of a household name—even in houses far from the beach!

Kelly was born in Florida, so being skilled at water sports seemed to come naturally to him. He won 10 major amateur titles, including four U.S. championships—all while he was still a teen!

In 1992, his first year on the world pro tour, he won the championship! At 21, he was the youngest title-winner ever! From then on, Kelly dominated the sport. He won a total of six **ASP Tour** World Championships, including five in a row (1994–98). No other man has even won four in a *career*!

ASP stands for Association of Surfing Professionals— surfers who earn money by winning surfing contests.

What made Kelly so good was his ability to ride any wave. He came up with moves no one had ever seen!

"Kelly Slater is to surfing what Tiger Woods is to golf," said surf writer Ben Marcus. "He is everything."

Then suddenly, in 1998, Slater **retired**! He wanted to travel, record music, be in movies, and have fun.

After a few years away from the surfing scene, however, Kelly felt the pull of the waves again. Proving that his time off hadn't hurt his surfing, Kelly won his seventh world title in 2005—and his eighth in 2006! At 33, Kelly was the oldest person to win the title!

As long as he climbs on his board, Kelly Slater will remain on top of the surfing world.

Off the Beach

Kelly Slater has used his fame and success in surfing to try out other ways to be a star. He had a regular role on the TV show *Baywatch*, which was about lifeguards in Santa Monica. He recorded an album with his rock group called The Surfers. He has appeared in numerous surfing videos, too.

While Kelly Slater's greatest rides make viewers on the beach go "Wow!", Laird Hamilton's rides leave watchers speechless. Hamilton is the "king of the big waves." He doesn't compete against other surfers, only against the ocean itself. Hamilton searches out the biggest waves the ocean can make, sometimes as high as 60 feet (18 m)!

Based in Hawaii, Hamilton invented "tow-in" surfing. In this version of the sport, surfers are pulled by small watercraft into the path of enormous waves. They strap their feet into clips on the board, and then zip down a roaring wave the size of a building.

Most tow-in surfers work with Jet Skis. These are like water scooters. Riders sit on top and steer with handlebars. They can go faster or slower with a hand control.

Hamilton's bravery and his ability to **merge** style and strength have made him a hero to many. His ride at a famous **surf break** in Tahiti is called one of the greatest ever.

Compare this wave Hamilton is riding to the ones on pages 7 or 10. Hamilton's one brave dude!

SURFER
Girls

Only one surfer can challenge Kelly Slater's record of world championships—Australian Layne Beachley. She has dominated women's surfing as much as Slater has controlled the men's side. Women have been surfing ever since Duke Kahanamoku hit the waves. In fact, the first surfer in Australia to ride with Duke was a woman, Isabel Letham.

Following in Isabel's wake, Layne started as a pro surfer in 1990. It took her a while to get hot, but once she did, she stayed that way. Layne won her first of six straight titles in 1998. After other surfers finally knocked her off the top in 2004, she showed that she's still got her surfing stuff. Layne won yet another world title in 2006. Her seven titles are just one short of Slater's record.

Layne is a member of both the U.S. and Australian Surfing Halls of Fame.

So who knocked Layne off the top spot in 2004? This champion wasn't from California, Hawaii, or Australia. Sofia Mulanovich learned to surf in the waves off her home country of Peru. She's one of many great surfers now coming from countries other than the traditional surfing homes.

Mulanovich started surfing at a very young age, and was the ASP Tour **rookie** of the year when she was only 20. At age 21 (in 2004), her second year as a pro, she became the first world surfing champ— male or female—from South America. She's been among the top scorers ever since, and has a cool "go-for-it" attitude.

Another South American surfer girl is Silvana Lima from Brazil. As a rookie in 2006, she got a perfect score of 10 on her first wave! The next year, she was among the leaders of the entire ASP Tour for most of the season. Silvana is a name you'll want to watch for in the future.

Sofia is not afraid to try a tricky cut-back move on the top of a wave.

Carissa's style is powerful and bold, and judges are taking notice.

Hawaii still produces top surfers, too. One young Hawaiian to watch is Carissa Moore. At just 16, she's already an amateur champion. In 2006, she won an event on the Rip Curl tour . . . competing against men and boys! She got a 10 in a 2007 event—also against men.

Carissa is following after another great Hawaiian surfer who's still out there competing. Megan Abubo has been on the ASP Tour since 1996, when she was the rookie of the year. Since then, she has won more than a dozen surfing events and has been **ranked** as high as number two. Although Australians hold most of the top spots these days, Megan remains one of America's best surfers.

One Brave Surfer

Bethany Hamilton was a top teen surfer in 2003, on her way to a pro career. But during a ride in Hawaii that year, she was attacked by a shark and lost an arm. She has battled back to continue her career, however!

TODAY'S SURFING Stars

Kelly Slater might still be out there, but lots of other surfers are trying to take his top spot. Here are a few super surfers to watch!

One who has already succeeded is the 2007 ASP Tour world champion Mick Fanning. This Australian started his pro-surfing career in 2002 and seemed ready to rocket to the top. But a bad fall in 2003 took him out of the sport for nearly two seasons. He worked hard to get better, and returned to prove that he was among the best.

In 2007, Mick finally reached the top. He won events in France, Brazil, and Australia. (That's one of the fun things about being a surfing star. You get to travel all over the world doing what you love!) He racked up enough points to clinch the championship. The surfer they call "White Lightning" for his quick moves was the first Australian champ since 1999.

Mick was down for a while, but he got back on his surfboard and reached the top of the ASP Tour.

Another Australian who's often in the hunt to take the top spot is Taj Burrow. His parents were from the United States and moved to Australia in search of great surfing. Taj was born there, and grew up with a surfboard on his feet.

He won his first big event when he was just nine years old. It didn't matter to Taj that all the other surfers in the event were teenagers!

Today, Taj thrills crowds and inspires young surfers with his amazing variety of **aerial** moves. Taj can glide up the face of a wave, rocket off the top, and do spins and flips before landing back on the wave—still surfing! Taj is perhaps

What do Shark Island, Winki Pop Bells, Gnarloo, and Noosa have in common? They're all popular Australian surf spots!

the best "big air" surfer on tour. Awesome!

While he gets lots of big air, Taj is still in search of the big one, as in number one. He was the rookie of the year in 1996, but three times since—1999, 2002, and 2007—Taj has finished as the ASP runner-up.

Look out below! Like a skateboarder, Taj sometimes grabs hold of his board during an aerial move.

Here's Andy Irons showing how to "shoot the curl"– riding under the wave as it breaks over his head!

Perhaps the only male surfer to come close to the great Kelly Slater has been Andy Irons. While Slater was on "retirement" in 2002, Andy won the world title. Even when Slater came back, Andy won two more world titles (in 2003 and 2004). He had to beat Slater in the final event of 2003 to keep his championship streak going.

Like many other great surfers, Andy grew up in Hawaii. He was on a board as soon as he could swim. And he always had someone to surf with—his younger brother Bruce.

In 2004, Bruce celebrated a win at a "big wave" event in Hawaii.

Andy joined the pro surfing tour in 1998 and Bruce came along in 2003. While Andy remains among the top surfers on the planet, Bruce hasn't had as much success—but few surfers have had as much fun as the easygoing Bruce.

Another American to watch is Bobby Martinez. Like Tom Curren, Bobby grew up in California. He won three events in his first two years as a pro.

Tall and strong, Australian Stephanie Gilmore is the next star to watch on the women's tour. In 2007 (her first year on the tour), she became the first woman to capture the world title as a rookie. With Layne Beachley getting older, will Stephanie become the next female superstar surfer?

On the men's side, watch for super rookie Jordy Smith. He set a record in 2007 while earning a place on the pro tour. He also signed a huge **contract** with a surf **sponsor**!

Surfing continues to grow in popularity around the world. Surfing shows up in TV shows and in movies, and you probably

use surfing language and don't even know it. Have you ever told someone to "hang loose"? That's from surfing.

From Hawaii to California to Australia, surfing is a hot sport. Now it's your turn to hit the beach and give it a try!

Stephanie Gilmore burst onto the surfing scene in 2007.

GLOSSARY

aerial a surfing trick that takes the surfer and the board above the water's surface

amateur an athlete who does a sport for fun, not for money

ASP Tour an organized league in which professional surfers compete; "ASP" stands for "Association of Surfing Professionals"

contract an agreement between an athlete and a sports company (the agreement states the athlete will work for the company)

elegant graceful and beautiful

exhibitions events designed to show off a sport

merge combine

professional an athlete who is paid to play a sport

ranked given a position such as first, second, third, and so on

retired stopped working or stopped playing a professional sport

rookie an athlete in his or her first season as a professional

sponsor a company that pays an athlete to promote its products

surf break a place to catch a wave

FIND OUT MORE

BOOKS

The Encyclopedia of Surfing
by Matt Warshaw (Harvest Books, 2005)
Just about everything you ever wanted to know about surfing can be found in this big book.

The Girl's Guide to Surfing
by Louise Southerden (Ballantine Books, 2005)
The author, a surfer from Australia, offers lots of tips for aspiring surfer girls.

Surfing
by Ben Mondy (Gareth Stevens Publishing, 2007)
A surfing writer gives young readers an introduction to the sport.

Waves!
by Drew Campion (Gibbs Smith, 2003)
Learn more about the world that surfers live in. This book tells how waves are made, how they are ridden, and where to find the best ones.

WEB SITES

Visit our Web site for lots of links about surfing and top surfers:
www.childsworld.com/links

Note to Parents, Teachers, and Librarians: We routinely check our Web links to make sure they're safe, active sites—so encourage your readers to check them out!

INDEX

Abubo, Megan, 21

ASP Tour, 11, 19, 22

Australia, 8, 16, 18, 21, 22-23, 24

Barrow, Taj, 24-25

Beach Boys, 4

Beachley, Layne, 16-17, 28

Brazil, 19, 23

Carroll, Corky, 7

Carroll, Tom, 8

Curren, Pat, 9

Curren, Tom, 9

Dora, Miki, 6, 7

Fanning, Mick 22-23

Gilmore, Stephanie, 28

Hamilton, Bethany, 21

Hamilton, Laird, 14-15

Hawaii, 6, 14, 18, 21

Irons, Andy, 26

Irons, Bruce, 27

Kahanamoku, Duke, 4-5, 16

Letham, Isabel, 16

Lima, Silvana, 19

Lopez, Gerry, 6

Martinez, Bobby, 27

Moore, Carissa, 20

Mulanovich, Sofia, 18-19

Noll, Greg, 6

Peru, 18

Richards, Mark, 8

Slater, Kelly, 10-11, 12-13

Smith, Jordy, 28

Tahiti, 15

K. C. KELLEY has written more than a dozen books on sports and other topics for young readers. He's never been brave enough to climb on a surfboard, but he enjoys watching the experts surf near his home in Santa Barbara, California.